TABLE OF CONTENTS

INTRODUCTION

PREFACE

ICC = INTERNATIONAL CRICKET COUNCIL

FORMAT OF ICC WORLD CUP

PRIZE MONEY FOR ICC 2023

HOW THE TEAMS QUALIFIED

10 TEAMS THAT QUALIFIED

ICC ODI WORLD CHAMPIONS

ICC ODI TEAM RANKING

ICC ODI PLAYERS RANKING

SCHEDULE OF ALL MATCHES

SCHEDULE OF A MATCH

ICC WORLD CUP MATCHES 5OCT- 22OCT

ICC WORLD CUP MATCHES 23OCT-12NOV

TEAM INDIA

TEAM PAKISTAN

TEAM AUSTRALIA

TEAM SOUTH AFRICA

TEAM ENGLAND

TEAM NEW ZEALAND

TEAM SRI LANKA

TEAM BANGLADESH

TEAM AFGHANISTAN

TEAM NETHERLANDS

TEAM INDIA FIXTURES

TEAM PAKISTAN FIXTURES

TEAM AUSTRALIA FIXTURES

TEAM SOUTH AFRICA FIXTURES

TEAM ENGLAND FIXTURES

TEAM NEW ZEALAND FIXTURES

TEAM SRI LANKA FIXTURES

TEAM BANGLADESH FIXTURES

TEAM AFGHANISTAN FIXTURES

TEAM NETHERLANDS FIXTURES

VENUES

FIXTURES AT AHMEDABAD

FIXTURES AT BANGALORE

FIXTURES AT CHENNAI

FIXTURES AT DELHI

FIXTURES AT DHARMSHALA

FIXTURES AT HYDERBAD

FIXTURES AT KOLKATA

FIXTURES AT LUCKNOW

FIXTURES AT MUMBAI

FIXTURES AT PUNE

COMMENTATORS

MATCH OFFICIALS

KEY POINTS OF PLAYING CONDITIONS

RESERVE DAYS

GROUND, WEATHER AND LIGHT

DRS AND TECHNOLOGY

SUBSTITUTE

MINIMUM OVER RATE REQUIREMENTS

PLAYER RANKINGS FAQS

MRF TYRES ICC PLAYER AND TEAM RANKINGS EXPLAINED

CRICKET

ICC REVENUE

ICC VISION

ICC OTHER PROGRAMS

BCCI

BCCI REVENUE

BCCI PAY PACKAGE

CRICKET GROUNDS REVENUE

ADVERTISERS LOVE CRICKET

ACKNOWLEDGEMENTS

INTRODUCTION

ICC is a global governing body for cricket representing 108 member countries.

ICC conducts MENS ODI CRICKET WORLD CUP once in 4 years.

2023 is the 13th edition of the world cup.

Host country is India.

No of countries participating is 10.

Each team plays 9 group matches.

No of venues is 10.

45 days to decide the world cup winner.

The 4 highest ranked teams in group stages will enter semi-finals.

Winner of semi-finals will play the world cup decider on 19th Nov.

Total of 48 world cup games will be held from 5th Oct to 19th Nov, across 10 venues.

Star sports network will telecast in India

Disney + Hot star will live stream.

The ICC World Cup 2023 may boost host country India's economy by as much as USD 2.6 billion dollars.

PREFACE

Cricket owes much of its appeal and enjoyment to the fact that it should be played not only according to the Laws (which are incorporated within these Playing Conditions), but also within the Spirit of Cricket. The major responsibility for ensuring fair play rests with the captains, but extends to all players, match officials, coaches and parents.

Respect is central to the Spirit of Cricket. Respect your captain, team-mates, opponents and the authority of the umpires. Play hard and play fair. Accept the umpire's decision. Create a positive atmosphere by your own conduct, and encourage others to do likewise. Show self-discipline, even when things go against you. Congratulate the opposition on their successes, and enjoy those of your own team. Thank the officials and your opposition at the end of the match, whatever the result. Cricket is an exciting game that encourages leadership

Cricket is an exciting game that encourages leadership, friendship and teamwork, which brings together people from different nationalities, cultures and religions, especially when played within the Spirit of Cricket.

CRICKET HAS A SPORT IS LOOKINT AT AN AMAZING AND PROSPEROUS AND VIBRANT FUTURE.

ICC = INTERNATIONAL CRICKET COUNCIL

ICC is the global governing body of cricket. It was founded as the Imperial Cricket Conference in 1909 by representatives from AUSTRALIA and ENGLAND and SOUTH AFRICA. It was renamed as the International Cricket Conference in 1965, and took up its current name in 1987. The ICC has its headquarters in Dubai, United Arab Emirates.

The ICC has 108 member nations currently: 12 Full Members that play Test matches, and 96 Associate Members. The ICC is responsible for the organisation and governance of cricket's major international tournaments, most notably the Cricket World Cup, T20 World Cup, and ICC World Test Championship.

It also appoints the umpires and referees that officiate at all Sanctioned Test matches, One Day Internationals and Twenty20 Internationals. It promulgates the ICC Code of Conduct, which sets professional standards of discipline for international cricket, and also co-ordinates action against corruption and match-fixing through its Anti-Corruption and Security Unit (ACSU).

The ICC does not control bilateral fixtures between member countries (which include all Test matches), and neither does it govern domestic cricket within member countries. It does not make or alter the laws of the game, which have remained under the governance of the Marylebone Cricket Club since 1788.

Connect with ICC:

www.facebook.com/icc

www.instagram.com/ICC

www.youtube.com/ICC

https://www.tiktok.com/@icc

www.twitter.com/ICC

www.icc-cricket.com

email= enquiries@icc-cricket.com

FORMAT OF ICC WORLD CUP

Each team will play against each other once in a single league stage.

The top 4 teams following the completion of 45 matches will qualify for the semi-finals.

Match Date	Match	IST	Venue
November 15, 2023	Semi-final 01 (1st v 4th)	2:00 PM	Wankhede Stadium, Mumbai
Match Date	Match	IST	Venue
November 16, 2023	Semi-final 02 (2nd v 3rd)	2:00 PM	Eden Gardens, Kolkata
Match Date	Match	IST	Venue
November 19, 2023	Final	2:00 PM	Narendra Modi Stadium, Ahmedabad

PRIZE MONEY FOR ICC 2023

The breakdown of prize money allocations is as follows in USD:

Stage	Rate US$	Total US$
Winner (1)	4,000,000	4,000,000
Runner-up (1)	2,000,000	2,000,000
Losing Semi-Finalist (2)	800,000	1,600,000
Teams eliminated after group stage (6)	100,000	600,000
Winner of each group stage match (45)	40,000	1,800,000
Total		10,000,000

The breakdown of prize money allocations is as follows in INR:

Stage	APPROX RATE INR	APPROX RATE INR
Winner (1)	33CRORES	33CRORES
Runner-up (1)	16.5CRORES	16.5CRORES
Losing Semi-Finalist (2)	6.6CRORES	13.2CRORES
Teams eliminated after group stage (6)	83LAKHS	4.9CRORES
Winner of each group stage match (45)	33LAKHS	14.85CRORES
Total		82.45CRORES

HOW THE TEAMS QUALIFIED

The 13th chapter of the ICC Men's Cricket World Cup will be played in India between October 05 to November 19, 2023.

10 teams will participate in the championship across 10 different venues. Two-time champions India earned automatic qualification as they are the hosts of the quadrennial event, while 5-time winners Australia, Afghanistan, South Africa, defending champs England, Pakistan, 2019 runners-up New Zealand and Bangladesh claimed their ticket after finishing in the top 8 in the ICC Cricket World Cup ODI Super League 2019-2023.

The remaining two places were filled via the ICC Cricket World Cup Qualifiers, which were held in Zimbabwe earlier this year. The 1996 world champions Sri Lanka and the NL finished as the top-2 teams in that tournament.

As per International Cricket Council rules, all the 10 teams must finalise their squads by September 28, otherwise they will have to seek the governing body's approval for any amendments.

10 TEAMS THAT QUALIFIED

SL NO	TEAM	ICC ODI RANK on 4TH OCT 2023	PREVIOUS BEST	CAPTAIN
1	AFGHANISTHAN	9	GROUP STAGE	HASHMATULLAH SHAHIDI
2	AUSTRALIA	3	WINNERS 1987, 1999, 2003, 2007, 2015	PAT CUMMINS
3	BANGLADESH	8	QUARTER FINALS	SHAKIB AL HASAN
4	ENGLAND	5	WINNER 2019	JOS BUTLER
5	INDIA	1	WINNER 1983, 2011	ROHIT SHARMA
6	NETHERLANDS	14	GROUP STAGE	SCOTT EDWARDS
7	NEW ZEALAND	6	RUNNERUP 2019	KANE WILLIAMSON
8	PAKISTAN	2	WINNER 1992	BABAR AZAM
9	SOUTH AFRICA	4	SEMIFINALS	TEMBA BAVUMA
10	SRI LANKA	7	WINNER 1996	DASUN SHANAKA

ICC ODI WORLD CHAMPIONS

ICC WORLD CUP EDITION	YEAR	ICC ODI WORLD CHAMPIONS
1	1975	WEST INDIES
2	1979	WEST INDIES
3	1983	INDIA
4	1987	AUSTRALIA
5	1992	PAKISTAN
6	1996	SRILANKA
7	1999	AUSTRALIA
8	2003	AUSTRALIA
9	2007	AUSTRALIA
10	2011	INDIA
11	2015	AUSTRALIA
12	2019	ENLAND
13	2023	

ICC ODI TEAM RANKING

SLNO	TEAM	ICC ODI RANKING on 4TH OCT 2023
1	INDIA	1
2	PAKISTAN	2
3	AUSTRALIA	3
4	SOUTH AFRICA	4
5	ENLAND	5
6	NEW ZELAND	6
7	SRI LANKA	7
8	BANGLADESH	8
9	AFGANISTHAN	9
10	NETHERLANDS	14

ICC ODI PLAYERS RANKING

ICC ODI RANKING ON 4TH OCT 2023	BATSMAN	CONUTRY	RATINGS
1	BABAR AZAM	PAKISTAN	857
2	SHUBNAM GILL	INDIA	839
3	RASSIE VAN DER	SOUTH AFRICA	743
ALL TIME ICC ODI RANKING	VIV RICHARDS	WEST INDIES	935
ICC ODI RANKING ON 4TH OCT 2023	BOWLER	CONUTRY	RATINGS
1	MD SIRAJ	INDIA	669
2	MUJEEB UR REHMAN	BANGLADESH	657
3	RASHID KHAN	AFGANISTAN	655
ALL TIME ICC ODI RANKING	JOEL GARNER	WEST INDIES	940
ICC ODI RANKING ON 4TH OCT 2023	ALL ROUNDER	CONUTRY	RATINGS
1	SHAKIB AL HASAN	BANGLADESH	349
2	MD NABI	AFGANISTAN	302
3	SIKANDAR RAZA	ZIMBABWE	287
ALL TIME ICC ODI RANKING	KAPIL DEV	INDIA	631

SCHEDULE OF ALL MATCHES

MATCH DATES	SUMMARY
5TH OCT TO 19TH NOV	46 DAYS
TOTAL NO OF MATCHES	45+2+1= 48
DAY MATCHES	6
DAY NIGHT MATCHES	42
5TH OCT	FIRST MATCH
12TH NOV	LAST GROUP STAGE MATCH
13-14TH NOV	RESERVE DAYS
15TH NOV	FIRST SEMI FINAL
16TH NOV	SECOND SEMI FINAL
17-18TH NOV	RESERVE DAYS
19TH NOV	FINALS
5TH OCT - 12TH NOV	MINIMUM OF ONE MATCH PER DAY
7TH OCT	2 MATCHES PER DAY
10TH OCT	2 MATCHES PER DAY
21ST OCT	2 MATCHES PER DAY
28TH OCT	2 MATCHES PER DAY
4TH NOV	2 MATCHES PER DAY
11TH NOV	2 MATCHES PER DAY

SCHEDULE OF A MATCH

HOURS OF PLAY: 7 HRS
2 SESSIONS
3.5HRS PER SESSION
30 MINUTES INTERVAL BETWEEN THE 2 SESSIONS
DAY MATCHES:
SESSION 1 = 10.30HRS - 14HRS
INTERVAL = 14HRS - 14.30HRS
SESSION 2 = 14.30HRS - 18HRS
DAY NIGHT MATCH:
SESSION 1 = 14HRS - 17.30HRS
INTERVAL = 17.30HRS - 18HRS
SESSION 2 = 18HRS - 21.30HRS
ICC TV COVERAGE:
PRE-MATCH SHOW
AN INNINGS INTERVAL PROGRAMME
POST MATCH WRAP UP
THE MATCH REFREE CAN REDUCE THE LENGTH OF THE INTERVAL WHEN IT IS APPROPRIATE TO DO SO. BUT THE MINIMUM INTERVAL WILL BE 10 MINUTES.

ICC WORLD CUP MATCHES

5OCT- 22OCT

SL NO	DATE	MATCH	IST	VENUE
1	Oct-05	Engand v New Zealand	2:00PM	Ahmedabad
2	Oct-06	Pakistan v Netherlands	2:00 PM	Hyderabad
3	Oct-07	Afghanistan v Bangladesh	10:30 AM	Dharamshala
4	Oct-07	South Africa v Sri Lanka	2:00 PM	Delhi
5	Oct-08	India v Australia	2:00 PM	Chennai
6	Oct-09	New Zealand v Netherlands	2:00 PM	Hyderabad
7	Oct-10	England v Bangladesh	10:30 AM	Dharamshala
8	Oct-10	Pakistan v Sri Lanka	2:00 PM	Hyderabad
9	Oct-11	India v Afghanistan	2:00 PM	Delhi
10	Oct-12	Australia v South Africa	2:00 PM	Lucknow
11	Oct-13	New Zealand v Bangladesh	2:00 PM	Chennai
12	Oct-14	India v Pakistan	2:00 PM	Ahmedabad
13	Oct-15	England v Afghanistan	2:00 PM	Delhi
14	Oct-16	Australia v Sri Lanka	2:00 PM	Lucknow
15	Oct-17	South Africa v Netherlands	2:00 PM	Dharamshala
16	Oct-18	Afghanistan v New Zealand	2:00 PM	Chennai
17	Oct-19	India v Bangladesh	2:00 PM	Pune
18	Oct-20	Australia v Pakistan	2:00 PM	Bangalore
19	Oct-21	Netherlands v Sri Lanka	2:00 PM	Lucknow
20	Oct-21	South Africa v England	2:00 PM	Mumbai
21	Oct-22	India v New Zealand	2:00 PM	Dharamshala
22	Oct-23	Afghanistan v Pakistan	2:00 PM	Chennai

ICC WORLD CUP MATCHES 23OCT-12NOV

SL NO	DATE	MATCH	IST	VENUE
23	Oct-24	South Africa v Bangladesh	2:00 PM	Mumbai
24	Oct-25	New Zealand v Australia	2:00 PM	Dharamshala
25	Oct-26	England v Sri Lanka	2:00 PM	Bangalore
26	Oct-27	South Africa v Pakistan	2:00 PM	Chennai
27	Oct-28	Australia v New Zealand	10:30 AM	Dharamshala
28	Oct-28	Netherlands v Bangladesh	2:00 PM	Kolkata
29	Oct-29	India v England	2:00 PM	Lucknow
30	Oct-30	Afghanistan v Sri Lanka	2:00 PM	Pune
31	Oct-31	Pakistan v Bangladesh	2:00 PM	Kolkata
32	Nov-01	South Africa v New Zealand	2:00 PM	Pune
33	Nov-02	India v Sri Lanka	2:00 PM	Mumbai
34	Nov-03	Afghanistan v Netherland	2:00 PM	Lucknow
35	Nov-04	New Zealand v Pakistan	10:30 AM	Bangalore
36	Nov-04	England v Australia	2:00 PM	Ahmedabad
37	Nov-05	India v South Africa	2:00 PM	Kolkata
38	Nov-06	Bangladesh v Sri Lanka	2:00 PM	Delhi
39	Nov-07	Afghanistan v Australia	2:00 PM	Mumbai
40	Nov-08	NL v England	2:00 PM	Pune
41	Nov-09	New Zealand v Sri Lanka	2:00 PM	Bangalore
42	Nov-10	South Africa-Afghanistan	2:00 PM	Ahmedabad
43	Nov-11	Australia v Bangladesh	10:30 PM	Pune
44	Nov-11	England v Pakistan	2:00 PM	Kolkata
45	Nov-12	India v New Zeeland	2:00 PM	Bangalore

TEAM INDIA

Captain: Rohit Sharma Head Coach: Rahul Dravid

NAME	ROLE
ROHIT SHARMA (C)	BATSMAN
SHUBMAN GILL	BATSMAN
VIRAT KOHLI	BATSMAN
SHREYAS IYER	BATSMAN
KL RAHUL	BATSMAN
SURYAKUMAR YADAV	BATSMAN
ISHAN KISHAN	WICKETKEEPER / BATSMAN
HARDIK PANDYA (VC)	ALL ROUNDER
RAVINDRA JADEJA	ALL ROUNDER
AXAR PATEL	ALL ROUNDER
SHARDUL THAKUR	BOWLER
JASPRIT BUMRAH	BOWLER
MOHAMMED SIRAJ	BOWLER
KULDEEP YADAV	BOWLER
MOHAMMED SHAMI	BOWLER

TEAM PAKISTAN

Captain: Babar Azam Head Coach: Grant Bradburn

NAME	ROLE
BABAR AZAM (C)	BATSMAN
ABDULLAH SHAFIQUE	BATSMAN
FAKHAR ZAMAN	BATSMAN
IFTIKHAR AHMED	BATSMAN
IMAM-UL-HAQ	BATSMAN
MOHAMMAD RIZWAN	WICKETKEEPER/BATSMAN
SAUD SHAKEEL	BATSMAN
AGHA SALMAN	ALL-ROUNDER
MOHAMMAD NAWAZ	ALL-ROUNDER
MOHAMMAD WASIM	ALL-ROUNDER
SHADAB KHAN	ALL-ROUNDER
HARIS RAUF	BOWLER
SHAHEEN AFRIDI	BOWLER
HASAN ALI	BOWLER
USAMA MIR	BOWLER

TEAM AUSTRALIA

Captain: Pat Cummins Head Coach: Andrew McDonald

NAME	ROLE
PAT CUMMINS ©	BOWLER
STEVE SMITH	BATSMAN
ALEX CAREY	WICKETKEEPER-BATSMAN
JOSH INGLIS	WICKETKEEPER-BATSMAN
DAVID WARNER	BATSMAN
TRAVIS HEAD	BATSMAN
MITCHELL STARC	BOWLER
JOSH HAZLEWOOD	BOWLER
GLENN MAXWELL	BATTING ALL-ROUNDER
MARCUS STOINIS	BATTING ALL-ROUNDER
CAMERON GREEN	BATTING ALL-ROUNDER
ADAM ZAMPA	BOWLER
ASHTON AGAR	BOWLER
MITCH MARSH	BATTING ALL-ROUNDER
SEAN ABBOTT	BOWLER

TEAM SOUTH AFRICA

Captain: Temba Bavuma

Head Coach: Rob Walter

NAME	ROLE
TEMBA BAVUMA	BATSMAN
REEZA HENDRICKS	BATSMAN
DAVID MILLER	BATSMAN
RASSIE VAN DER DUSSEN	BATSMAN
QUINTON DE KOCK	WICKETKEEPER/BATSMAN
HEINRICH KLAASEN	WICKETKEEPER/BATSMAN
MARCO JANSEN	ALLROUNDER
AIDEN MARKRAM	ALLROUNDER
GERALD COETZEE	BOWLER
SISANDA MAGALA	BOWLER
KESHAV MAHARAJ	BOWLER
LUNGI NGIDI	BOWLER
ANRICH NORTJE	BOWLER
KAGISO RABADA	BOWLER
TABRAIZ SHAMSI	BOWLER

TEAM ENGLAND

Captain: Jos Buttler Head Coach: Matthew Motts

NAME	ROLE
JOS BUTTLER ©	WICKETKEEPER-BATSMAN
BEN STOKES	BATSMAN
JOE ROOT	BATSMAN
JONNY BAIRSTOW	WICKETKEEPER-BATSMAN
HARRY BROOK	BATSMAN
DAWID MALAN	BATSMAN
LIAM LIVINGSTONE	BATTING ALL-ROUNDER
SAM CURRAN	BOWLING ALL-ROUNDER
CHRIS WOAKES	BOWLER
MOEEN ALI	ALL-ROUNDER
ADIL RASHID	BOWLER
REECE TOPLEY	BOWLER
MARK WOOD	BOWLER
GUS ATKINSON	BOWLER
DAVID WILLEY	BOWLER

TEAM NEW ZEALAND

Captain: Kane Williamson Head Coach: Gary Stead

NAME	ROLE
KANE WILLIAMSON ©	BATSMAN
TOM LATHAM	WICKETKEEPER-BATSMAN
DEVON CONWAY	BATSMAN
DARYL MITCHELL	BATSMAN
GLENN PHILLIPS	BATSMAN
WILL YOUNG	BATSMAN
MARK CHAPMAN	BATSMAN
TRENT BOULT	BOWLER
TIM SOUTHEE	BOWLER
LOCKIE FERGUSON	BOWLER
MATT HENRY	BOWLER
MITCHELL SANTNER	BOWLER
ISH SODHI	BOWLER
JAMES NEESHAM	ALL-ROUNDER
RACHIN RAVINDRA	BOWLER

TEAM SRI LANKA

Captain: Dasun Shanaka Head Coach: Chris Silverwood

PLAYER NAME	ROLE
DASUN SHANAKA	ALL-ROUNDER
KUSAL MENDIS	WICKET-KEEPER
PATHUM NISSANKA	BATSMAN
DIMUTH KARUNARATNE	BATSMAN
SADEERA SAMARAWICKRAMA	WICKET-KEEPER
CHARITH ASALANKA	BATSMAN
DHANANJAYA DE SILVA	ALL-ROUNDER
KUSAL PERERA	WICKET-KEEPER
MAHEESH THEEKSHANA	BOWLER
DUNITH WELLALAGE	BOWLER
KASUN RAJITHA	BOWLER
MATHEESHA PATHIRANA	BOWLER
LAHIRU KUMARA	BOWLER
DILSHAN MADHUSHANKA	BOWLER
DUSHAN HEMANTHA	BOWLER

TEAM BANGLADESH

Captain: Shakib Al Hasan　　　Head Coach: Chandika

PLAYERS	ROLE
SHAKIB AL HASAN	ALL-ROUNDER
NAJMUL HOSSAIN	BATSMAN
LITTON DAS	WICKETKEEPER/BATSMAN
MUSHFIQUR RAHIM	WICKETKEEPER/BATSMAN
HASAN	BATSMAN
TOWHID HRIDOY	BATSMAN
MAHEDI HASAN	ALL-ROUNDER
MAHMUDULLAH	ALL-ROUNDER
MEHIDY HASAN MIRAZ	ALL-ROUNDER
TASKIN AHMED	BOWLER
MUSTAFIZUR RAHMAN	BOWLER
HASAN MAHMUD	BOWLER
NASUM AHMED	BOWLER
SHORIFUL ISLAM	BOWLER
HASAN SAKIB	BOWLER

TEAM AFGHANISTAN

Captain: Hashmatullah Shahidi - Head Coach: Jonathan Trott

PLAYERS	ROLE
HASHMATULLAH SHAHIDI	BATSMAN
IBRAHIM ZADRAN	BATSMAN
IKRAM ALIKHIL	WICKETKEEPER/BATSMAN
RAHMANULLAH GURBAZ	WICKETKEEPER/BATSMAN
NAJIBULLAH ZADRAN	BATSMAN
RIAZ HASAN	BATSMAN
AZMATULLAH OMARZAI	ALL-ROUNDER
MOHAMMAD NABI	ALL-ROUNDER
RAHMAT SHAH	ALL-ROUNDER
RASHID KHAN	BOWLER
RAHMAN	BOWLER
FAZALHAQ FAROOQI	BOWLER
NAVEEN-UL-HAQ	BOWLER
MUJEEB UR RAHMAN	BOWLER
NOOR AHMAD	BOWLER

TEAM NETHERLANDS

Captain: Scott Edwards Head Coach: Ryan ten Doeschate

NAME	ROLE
SCOTT EDWARDS ©	WICKETKEEPER-BATSMAN
MAX O'DOWD	ALL-ROUNDER
VIKRAMJIT SINGH	BATSMAN
TEJA NIDAMANURU	ALL-ROUNDER
WESLEY BARRESI	WICKETKEEPER-BATSMAN
COLIN ACKERMANN	ALL-ROUNDER
BAS DE LEEDE	ALL-ROUNDER
SHARIZ AHMAD	ALL-ROUNDER
ROELOF VAN DER MERVE	ALL-ROUNDER
LOGAN VAN BEEK	BOWLER
RYAN KLEIN	ALL-ROUNDER
ARYAN DUTT	ALL-ROUNDER
PAUL VAN MEEKEREN	ALL-ROUNDER
SYBRAND ENELBRECHT	BATSMAN
SAQIB ZULFIQAR	BATSMAN

TEAM INDIA FIXTURES

SLNO	DAY	DATE	CITY	OPPONENT
1	SUN	8TH OCT	CHENNAI	AUSTRALIA
2	WED	11TH OCT	DELHI	AFGHANISTAN
3	SUN	14TH OCT	AHMEDABAD	PAKISTAN
4	THU	19TH OCT	PUNE	BANGLADESH
5	SUN	22ND OCT	DHARMSHALA	NEW ZEALAND
6	SUN	29TH OCT	LUCKNOW	ENGLAND
7	THU	2ND NOV	MUMBAI	SRILANKA
8	SUN	5TH NOV	KOLKATA	SOUTH AFRICA
9	SAT	12TH NOV	BANGALORE	NETHERLANDS

TEAM PAKISTAN FIXTURES

SLNO	DAY	DATE	CITY	OPPONENT
1	FRI	6TH OCT	HYDERABAD	NETHERLANDS
2	TUE	10TH OCT	HYDERABAD	SRILANKA
3	SAT	14TH OCT	AHMEDABAD	INDIA
4	FRI	20TH OCT	BANGALORE	AUSTRALIA
5	MON	23RD OCT	CHENNAI	AFGHANISTAN
6	FRI	27TH OCT	CHENNAI	SOUTH AFRICA
7	TUE	31ST OCT	KOLKATA	BANGLADESH
8	SAT	4TH NOV	BANGALORE	NEW ZEALAND
9	SAT	11TH NOV	KOLKATA	ENGLAND

TEAM AUSTRALIA FIXTURES

SLNO	DAY	DATE	CITY	OPPONENT
1	SUN	8TH OCT	CHENNAI	INDIA
2	FRI	12THOCT	LUCKNOW	SOUTH AFRICA
3	MON	16TH OCT	LUCKNOW	SRILANKA
4	FRI	20TH OCT	BANGALORE	PAKISTAN
5	WED	25TH OCT	DELHI	NETHERLANDS
6	SAT	28TH OCT	DHARMSHALA	NEW ZEALAND
7	SAT	4TH NOV	AHMEDABAD	ENGLAND
8	TUE	7TH NOV	MUMBAI	AFGHANISTAN
9	SUN	11TH NOV	PUNE	BANGLADESH

TEAM SOUTH AFRICA FIXTURES

SLNO	DAY	DATE	CITY	OPPONENT
1	SAT	7TH OCT	DELHI	SRILANKA
2	THU	12TH OCT	LUCKNOW	AUSTRALIA
3	TUE	17TH OCT	DHARMSHALA	NETHERLANDS
4	SAT	21ST OCT	MUMBAI	ENGLAND
5	TUE	24TH OCT	MUMBAI	BANGLADESH
6	FRI	27TH OCT	CHENNAI	PAKISTAN
7	WED	1ST NOV	PUNE	NEW ZEALAND
8	SUN	5TH NOV	KOLKATA	INDIA
9	FRI	10TH NOV	AHMEDABAD	AFGHANISTAN

TEAM ENGLAND FIXTURES

SLNO	DAY	DATE	CITY	OPPONENT
1	THU	5TH OCT	AHMEDABAD	NEW ZEALAND
2	TUE	10TH OCT	DHARMSHALA	BANGLADESH
3	SUN	15TH OCT	DELHI	AFGHANISTAN
4	SAT	21ST OCT	MUMBAI	SOUTH AFRICA
5	THU	26TH OCT	BANGALORE	SRI LANKA
6	SUN	29TH OCT	LUCKNOW	INDIA
7	SAT	4TH NOV	AHMEDABAD	AUSTRALIA
8	WED	8TH NOV	PUNE	NETHERLANDS
9	SAT	11TH NOV	KOLKATA	PAKISTAN

TEAM NEW ZEALAND FIXTURES

SLNO	DAY	DATE	CITY	OPPONENT
1	THU	5TH OCT	AHMEDABAD	ENGLAND
2	MON	9TH OCT	HYDERABAD	NETHERLANDS
3	FRI	13TH OCT	CHENNAI	BANGLADESH
4	WED	18TH OCT	CHENNAI	AFGHANISTAN
5	SUN	22ND OCT	DHARMSHALA	INDIA
6	SAT	28TH OCT	DHARMSHALA	AUSTRALIA
7	WED	1ST NOV	PUNE	SOUTH AFRICA
8	SAT	4TH NOV	BANGALORE	PAKISTAN
9	THU	9TH NOV	BANGALORE	SRILANKA

TEAM SRI LANKA FIXTURES

SLNO	DAY	DATE	CITY	OPPONENT
1	SAT	7TH OCT	DELHI	SOUTH AFRICA
2	TUE	10TH OCT	HYDERABAD	PAKISTAN
3	MON	16TH OCT	LUCKNOW	AUSTRALIA
4	SAT	21ST OCT	LUCKNOW	NETHERLANDS
5	THU	26TH OCT	BANGALORE	ENGLAND
6	MON	30TH OCT	PUNE	AFGHANISTAN
7	THU	2ND NOV	MUMBAI	INDIA
8	MON	6TH NOV	DELHI	BANGLADESH
9	THU	9TH NOV	BANGALORE	NEW ZEALAND

TEAM BANGLADESH FIXTURES

SLNO	DAY	DATE	CITY	OPPONENT
1	SAT	7TH OCT	DHARMSHALA	AFGHANISTAN
2	TUE	10TH OCT	DHARMSHALA	ENGLAND
3	FRI	13TH OCT	CHENNAI	NEW ZEALAND
4	THU	19TH OCT	PUNE	INDIA
5	TUE	24TH OCT	MUMBAI	SOUTH AFRICA
6	SAT	28TH OCT	KOLKATA	NETHERLANDS
7	TUE	31ST OCT	KOLKATA	PAKISTAN
8	MON	6TH NOV	DELHI	SRILANKA
9	SUN	12TH NOV	PUNE	AUSTRALIA

TEAM AFGHANISTAN FIXTURES

SLNO	DAY	DATE	CITY	OPPONENT
1	SAT	7THOCT	DHARMSHALA	BANGLADESH
2	WED	11TH OCT	DELHI	INDIA
3	SUN	15TH OCT	DELHI	ENGLAND
4	WED	18TH OCT	CHENNAI	NEW ZEALAND
5	MON	23RD OCT	CHENNAI	PAKISTAN
6	MON	30TH OCT	PUNE	SRILANKA
7	FRI	3RD NOV	LUCKNOW	NETHERLANDS
8	TUE	7TH NOV	MUMBAI	AUSTRALIA
9	FRI	1OTH NOV	AHMEDABAD	SOUTH AFRICA

TEAM NETHERLANDS FIXTURES

SLNO	DAY	DATE	CITY	OPPONENT
1	FRI	6TH OCT	HYDERABAD	PAKISTAN
2	MON	9TH OCT	HYDERABAD	NEW ZEALAND
3	TUE	17TH OCT	DHARMSHALA	SOUTH AFRICA
4	SAT	21ST OCT	LUCKNOW	SRILANKA
5	WED	25TH OCT	DELHI	AUSTRALIA
6	SAT	28TH OCT	KOLKATTA	BANGLADESH
7	FRI	3RD NOV	LUCKNOW	AFGHANISTAN
8	WED	8TH NOV	PUNE	ENGLAND
9	SUN	12TH NOV	BANGALORE	INDIA

VENUES

SLNO	CITY	NAME OF STADIUM	NO OF MATCHES
1	AHMEDABAD	NARENDRA MODI STADIUM	5
2	BANGALORE	M CHINNASWAMY STADIUM	5
3	CHENNAI	MA CHIDAMBARAM STADIUM	5
4	DELHI	ARUN JAITLEY STADIUM	5
5	DHARMSHALA	HPCA STADIUM	5
6	HYDERABAD	RAJIV GANDHI STADIUM	3
7	KOLKATTA	EDEN GARDENS	5
8	LUCKNOW	BRSABVE STADIUM	5
9	MUMBAI	WANKHEDE STADIUM	5
10	PUNE	MCA INTERNATIONAL STADIUM	5
			TOTAL=48

FIXTURES AT AHMEDABAD

SLNO	DAY	DATE	TIME	MATCHES
1	THU	5TH OCT	2PM	NEW ZEALAND VS ENGLAND
2	SAT	14TH OCT	2PM	INDIS VS PAKISTAN
3	SAT	4TH NOV	2PM	ENGLAND VS AUSTRALIA
4	FRI	10TH NOV	2PM	SOUTH AFRICA VS AFGHANISTAN
5	SUN	19TH NOV	2PM	FINALS

FIXTURES AT BANGALORE

SLNO	DAY	DATE	TIME	PLACE
1	FRI	20TH OCT	2PM	AUSTRALIA VS PAKISTAN
2	THU	26TH OCT	2PM	ENGLAND VS SRILANKA
3	SAT	4TH NOV	10.30AM	NEW ZEALAND VS PAKISTAN
4	THU	9TH NOV	2PM	NEW ZEALAND VS SRI LANKA
5	SUN	12TH NOV	2PM	INDIA VS NETHERLANDS

FIXTURES AT CHENNAI

SLNO	DAY	DATE	TIME	PLACE
1	SUN	8TH OCT	2PM	INDIA VS AUSTRALIA
2	FRI	13TH OCT	2PM	NEW ZEALAND VS BANGLADESH
3	WED	18TH OCT	2PM	NEW ZEALAND VS AFGHANISTAN
4	MON	23RD OCT	2PM	PAKISTAN VS AFGHANISTAN
5	FRI	27TH OCT	2PM	INDIA VS SOUTH AFRICA

FIXTURES AT DELHI

SLNO	DAY	DATE	TIME	PLACE
1	SAT	7TH OCT	2PM	SOUTH AFRICA VS SRI LANKA
2	WED	11TH OCT	2PM	INDIA VS AFGHANISTAN
3	SUN	15TH OCT	2PM	ENGLAND VS AFGHANISTAN
4	WED	25TH OCT	2PM	AUSTRALIA VS NETHARLANDS
5	MON	6TH NOV	2PM	BANGLADESH VS SRILANKA

FIXTURES AT DHARMSHALA

SLNO	DAY	DATE	TIME	PLACE
1	SAT	7TH OCT	10.30AM	BANGLADESH VS AFGHANISTAN
2	TUE	10TH OCT	10.30AM	BANGLADESH VS ENGLAND
3	TUE	17TH OCT	2PM	SOUTH AFRICA VS NETHERLANDS
4	SUN	22ND OCT	2PM	INDIA VS NEW ZEALAND
5	SAT	28TH OCT	10.30AM	AUSTRALIA VS NEW ZEALAND

FIXTURES AT HYDERBAD

SLNO	DAY	DATE	TIME	PLACE
1	FRI	6TH OCT	2PM	PAKISTAN VS NETHERLANDS
2	MON	9TH OCT	2PM	NEW ZEALAND VS NETHERLANDS
3	TUE	10TH OCT	2PM	PAKISTAN VS SRI LANKA

FIXTURES AT KOLKATA

SLNO	DAY	DATE	TIME	PLACE
1	SAT	28TH OCT	2PM	NETHERLANDS VS BANGLADESH
2	TUE	31ST OCT	2PM	PAKISTAN VS BANGLADESH
3	SUN	5TH NOV	2PM	INDIA VS SOUTH AFRICA
4	SAT	11TH NOV	2PM	ENGLAND VS PAKISTAN
5	THU	16TH NOV	2PM	SEMI- FINAL 2

FIXTURES AT LUCKNOW

SLNO	DAY	DATE	TIME	PLACE
1	THU	12TH OCT	2PM	AUSTRALIA VS SOUTH AFRICA
2	MON	16TH OCT	2PM	AUSTRALIA VS SRI LANKA
3	SAT	21ST OCT	10.30AM	NETHERLANDS VS SRI LANKA
4	SUN	29TH OCT	2PM	INDIA VS ENGLAND
5	FRI	3RD NOV	2PM	NETHERLANDS VS AFGHANISTAN

FIXTURES AT MUMBAI

SLNO	DAY	DATE	TIME	PLACE
1	SAT	21ST OCT	2PM	ENGLAND VS SOUTH AFRICA
2	TUE	24TH OCT	2PM	SOUTH AFRICA VS BANGLADESH
3	THU	2ND NOV	2PM	INDIA VS SRILANKA
4	TUE	7TH NOV	2PM	AUSTRALIA VS AFGHANISTAN
5	WED	15TH NOV	2PM	SEMI FINAL 1

FIXTURES AT PUNE

SLNO	DAY	DATE	TIME	PLACE
1	THU	19TH OCT	2PM	INDIS VS BANGLADESH
2	MON	30TH OCT	2PM	AFGHANISTAN VS SRI LANKA
3	WED	1ST NOV	2PM	NEW ZEALAND VS SOUTH AFRICA
4	WED	8TH NOV	2PM	ENGLAND VS NETHERLANDS
5	SAT	11TH NOV	2PM	AUSTRALIA VS BANGLADESH

COMMENTATORS

COUNTRY	FORMER PLAYERS AS COMMENTATORS	TOTAL
AUSTRALIA	RICKY PONTING, SHANE WATSON, MATTHEW HAYDEN, AARON FINCH, LISA STHALEKAR	6
BANGLADESH	ATHAR ALI KHAN	2
ENGLAND	EOIN MORGAN, MICHAEL ATHERTON, NASSER HUSSAIN	3
INDIA	ANJUM CHOPRA, RAVI SHASTRI, SUNIL GAVASKAR, DINESH KARTHIK, SANJAY MANJREKAR	5
NEW ZEALAND	IAN SMITH, KATEY MARTIN, SIMON DOULL	3
PAKISTAN	RAMIZ RAJA, WAQAR YOUNIS	2
SOUTH AFRICA	SHAUN POLLOCK	1
SRI LANKA	RUSSEL ARNOLD	1
WEST INDIES	SAMUEL BADREE, IAN BISHOP	2
ZIMBABWE	MPUMELELO MBANGWA	1
		26
COUNTRY	BROADCASTERS AS COMMENTATORS	TOTAL
AUSTRALIA	NATALIE GERMANOS, MARK HOWARD	2
ENGLAND	MARK NICHOLAS, IAN WARD	2
INDIA	HARSHA BHOGLE	1
SOUTH AFRICA	KASS NAIDOO	1
		6

MATCH OFFICIALS

UMPIRES	MATCH REFREES	UMPIRE COACHES
ADRIAN HOLDSTOCK	ANDY PYCROFT	DAVID LEVENS
AHSAN RAZA	JAVGAL SRINATH	KARL HURTER
ALEX WHARF	JEFF CROWE	PETER MANUEL
CHRIS BROWN	RICHIE RICHARDSON	STUART CUMMINGS
CHRIS GAFFANEY		
JOEL WILSON		
KUMAR DHARMASENA		
MARIAS ERASMUS		
MICHAEL GOUGH		
NITIN MENON		
PAUL REIFFEL		
PAUL WILSON		
RICHARD ILLINGWORTH		
RICHARD KETTLEBOROUGH		
ROD TUCKER		
SHARFUDDOULA IBNE SHAID		

KEY POINTS OF PLAYING CONDITIONS

STANDARD ODI PLAYING CONDITIONS APPLY TO ALL GAMES IN ICC 2023 WORLD CUP MATCHES

HOURS OF PLAY:

2SESSIONS

3.5HRS PER SESSION

30 MINUTES INTERVAL BETWEEN THE 2 SESIONS

DAY MATCHES:

SESSION 1 = 10.30HRS - 14HRS

INTERVAL = 14HRS - 14.30HRS

SESSION 2 = 14.30HRS - 18HRS

DAY NIGHT MATCH:

SESSION 1 = 14HRS - 17.30HRS

INTERVAL = 17.30HRS - 18HRS

SESSION 2 = 18HRS - 21.30HRS

The match referee can reduce the length of the interval when it is appropriate to do so, but the minimum interval will be 10 minutes.

60 minutes of extra time can be allocated to all matches.

120 minutes of extra can be allocated to semi-finals and final matches.

A super over - or multiple super overs - will be played to determine the result of any tied match.

RESERVE DAYS

Only semi-finals and finals will have reserve day allocated on which an incomplete match shall be continued from the scheduled day.

Only if the minimum number of overs necessary to constitute a match cannot be bowled on the scheduled day only then will the match be completed on the reserve day.

If the match has started on the scheduled day and overs are subsequently reduced following an interruption, but no further play is possible, the match will resume on the reserve day at the point where the last ball was played.

GROUND, WEATHER AND LIGHT

Umpires will maximise play at all times and expect teams to do also.

Umpires are the sole judge of ground, weather and light issues.

Where lightning threatens or air pollution is assessed as problematic the umpires will consider suspending play to ensure participant safety.

Uncomfortable and unsafe conditions will be considered to start or suspension of play.

Who decides how good the pitch is? Nobody does. There is a common misconception that there is an expert panel that sits down to assess the pitch in each match.

DRS AND TECHNOLOGY

Full Specification at All Matches

Auto No Ball

Ultra Edge with Split Screen

Clean Audio Feed

LED Wickets

- 2 unsuccessful DRS reviews allowed per team per innings.
- A review will be retained if umpires call against the review.
- After referral to the third umpire, the 3rd umpire decision will be given on the big screen.
- The 3rd will check for front foot no ball immediately after each delivery.
- If checking for a fair delivery after a dismissal, the 3rd umpire can check for all forms of no ball on request except for illegal bowling action.

The Decision Review System (DRS), formerly known as the Umpire Decision Review System (UDRS), is a technology-based system used in cricket to assist the match officials in their decision-making. On-field umpires may choose to consult with the third umpire (known as an Umpire Review), and players may request that the third umpire consider a decision of the on-field umpires (known as a Player Review).

The main elements that have been used are television replays, technology that tracks the path of the ball and predicts what it would have done, microphones to detect small sounds made as the ball hits bat or pad, and infra-red imaging to detect temperature changes as the ball hits the bat or pad.

While on-field Test match umpires have been able to refer some decisions to a third umpire since November 1992, the formal DRS system to add Player Reviews was first used in a Test match in 2008, first used in a One Day International (ODI) in January 2011, and used in a Twenty20 International in October 2017.

SUBSTITUTE

Any substitute or replacement player must be an official squad member of the team.

Team to request for a replacement via a match referee.

Match referee cannot approve changes to a team's official squad only event technical committee can.

MINIMUM OVER RATE REQUIREMENTS

Fielding teams must comply with over rate requirements.

Pace of play protocols are to be observed.

No changing of bats and gloves between overs unless permission is granted by on field umpires.

If batting team unnecessarily delays play then they can expect the umpires to take action like reduction in that teams bowling innings allowances.

If teams huddle before the start of a session or after a drink break, time will start when the umpires are ready.

Over rates will be displayed continuously and in match fielding restrictions penalties will be applied as required.

Incoming batsman are expected to be ready within 120 seconds. If they are late, they will be timed out.

PLAYER RANKINGS FAQS

- What do the rankings measure?
- Think of the MRF Tyres ICC Rankings as a system for identifying the players who could be selected for an ICC World XI if it was picked today. Take a look at the latest top ten, and you should find that most of the players at the top would be candidates for your current World XI. The rankings have often been described as a measure of form, but this is a simplification. A form ranking would only look at what a player has done in (Say) the last year, whereas rankings take into account a player's entire career - though more emphasis on what the player has done recently.
- What's the difference between 'rankings' and 'ratings?
- Rankings to refer to the positions of players in the tables, and 'ratings' to refer to their points.
- How do you decide who is or isn't included in the list?
- Players have to have appeared in a match within the qualifying period to appear in the lists (normally 12-15 months for Tests, 9 -12 months for T20s and ODIs).
- When are the rankings updated?
- For men across all three formats – Tests, ODIs and T20Is – are updated on Wednesdays. These updates include all matches completed till the previous day and do not include any matches played on the day of updating. The team rankings continue to be updated as before – after each Test series and after each ODI and T20I.
- What happens to a player's rating if he plays but does not bat/bowl?
- If a batsman does not bat, his rating is unchanged.

- What does it mean to have, Say, 500 points?
- Ratings points have a meaning in the same way as traditional averages do. Over 900 points is a supreme achievement. Few players get there, and even fewer stay there for long. 750 plus is normally enough to put a player in the world top ten. 500 plus is a good, solid rating.
- What about ratings for wicket-keepers?
- There is no Satisfactory way of rating wicket keeping skills statistically at present.
- Who decides how good the pitch is?
- If both teams score 500 in each innings, the computer rates this as a high-scoring match in which run-making was relatively easy, and therefore downgrades the value of runs scored. If both teams score 150, this Indicates that runs were at a premium and a player gets greater credit for scoring well in this game.
- How do you rate all-rounders?
- ICC has devised an all-rounder Index that gives a good Indication of who the best all-rounders in the world are in Test and One Day cricket. To obtain the Index, simply take the player's batting and bowling points, multiply them together and divide by 1000. So, a player with 800 batting and 0 bowling gets an Index of zero (clausthalite he can't bowl and therefore isn't an all-rounder!), 600 batting/200 bowling gets a rating of 120, and 400 batting/400 bowling points gets a rating of 160. An Index of 300 plus is world class. There are far more all-rounders in T20s and ODIs than Tests, but the Same names tend to appear high in both lists. Incidentally, this Index does omit one important all-rounder skill, namely fielding. There is no Satisfactory way of rating fielding skills statistically at present.

- Is it harder to score points against some of the lower ranked teams than it might be to score points against the higher teams?
- Because the ratings take account of the opposition strength, there shouldn't be any obvious advantage to playing against any particular team. Of course, that's not to say that certain individuals do seem to play better against certain opposition or on certain types of pitch.

MRF TYRES ICC PLAYER AND TEAM RANKINGS EXPLAINED

The MRF Tyres ICC Player Rankings is a table where international cricket players performances are ranked using a points-based system which is worked out by doing a series of calculations leading to a sophisticated moving average. Players are rated on a scale of 0 to 1000 points. If a player's performance is improving on his past record, his points increase; if the players performance is declining his points will go down. The value of each player's performance within a match is calculated using an algorithm, a series of calculations (all pre-programmed) based on various circumstances in the match. There is no human intervention in this calculation process, and no subjective assessment is made. There are slightly different factors for each of the different formats of the game.

MRF Tyres ICC Team Rankings

The MRF Tyres ICC Team Rankings is a rating method developed by David Kendix to rank men's teams playing across Test, One-Day International and Twenty20 International formats This rating is worked out by dividing the points scored by the match/series total, with the answer given to the nearest whole number. It can be compared with a batting average, but with points instead of total runs scored and a match/series total instead of number of times dismissed.

CRICKET

Marylebone Cricket Club was founded in 1787, by the ambitious entrepreneur Thomas Lord.

The following year, MCC laid down a Code of Laws, requiring the wickets to be pitched 22 yards apart and detailing how players could be given out. Its Laws were adopted throughout the game – and the Club today remains the custodian and arbiter of Laws relating to cricket around the world.

And MCC recognize and have handed all powers except the laws to the ICC officially as part of their documents, which makes ICC legitimate International Cricket Body.

According to ICC CONSTITUTION its members must manage its affairs autonomously and ensure that there is no government (or other public or quasi-public body) interference in its governance, regulation and/or administration of Cricket in its Cricket Playing Country (including in operational matters, in the selection and management of teams, and in the appointment of coaches or support personnel).

It is a private body. As per ICC, all sports bodies must be Independent and autonomous and must not be under the control of the government

And ICC Recognizes BCCI as Representative of India since 1928.

ICC REVENUE

The ICC revenue model is quite complicated. Not each penny owned by the cricket-boards goes to the ICC. A fixed percentage of the profit earned goes to the ICC and the rest of the money is distributed between the host country and the visiting country. In tournaments like the ICC champions Trophy a major chunk of revenue goes to the International Cricket Council.

The various cricket boards are paid with respect to the amount of revenue they bring to the ICC. India AUSTRALIA and ENGLAND are the big three and hence a major chunk of revenue from the ICC goes to these countries because they bring a huge share of revenue to the international cricket council.

INDIAN cricket board contributes about 85.7 percentage of the total revenue and that's why a major chunk of revenue goes to INDIA.

The ICC generates income from the tournaments it organises, mainly the Cricket World Cup. Sponsorship and television rights of the World Cup brought in over US$1.6 billion between 2007 and 2015, by far the ICC's main source of income.

The ICC has no income streams from the international cricket matches like Test matches, One Day International and Twenty20 International, as they are owned and run by its members.

That was the reason why ICC created other new events which includes the ICC Champions Trophy and the ICC Super Series. But these events have not been as successful as the ICC hoped.

ICC earns money from their Global tournaments (ICC events).

Their major earning is in Gate receipts for these tournaments.

ICC VISION

Cricket is an exciting game that encourages leadership, friendship and teamwork, which brings together people from different nationalities, cultures and religions, especially when played within the Spirit of Cricket.

ICC TV's vision is to create and provide credible, informative and engaging live and non-live content, that speaks to a global audience, attracts new fans and in the long term helps position Cricket as the "World's Favourite Sport"

The ICC has a long-term ambition for cricket to become the world's favourite sport. ICC will lead the continued drive towards more competitive, entertaining, and meaningful cricket for players and fans. ICC will grow the sport by creating more opportunities for more people and nations to enjoy it and increase the competitiveness of international cricket at all levels. ICC will promote cricket by delivering exciting and engaging global events, attracting new and diverse fans, and building long-term successful commercial partnerships. And finally, ICC will continue to make considerable efforts to protect the integrity of the sport.

The strategic pillars of strengthen, grow, and protect will be underpinned by digital transformation of the sport to support members to connect directly with fans and build capacity.

Cricket is unique in that there are obligations within its Laws that require the captains, players and match officials to uphold the 'spirit of the sport'. The ICC, too, plays a significant role in protecting the spirit and integrity of the game through the ICC Code of Conduct, the efforts of our Anti-Corruption Unit (ACU), our Anti-Doping programme and our commitment to ensuring racism has no place in CRICKET.

ICC OTHER PROGRAMS

ICC CRICKET WORLD PROGRAM

The International Cricket Council telecasts a weekly program on television called ICC Cricket World. It is produced by Sports brand. It is a weekly 30-minute program providing the latest cricket news, recent cricket action including all Test and One-Day International matches, as well as off-field features and interviews.

ICC AWARDS

The ICC has instituted the ICC Awards to recognize and honour the best international cricket players of the previous 12 months. The inaugural ICC Awards ceremony was held on 7 September 2004, in London. In 2020, ICC announced a special one-off event, the ICC Awards of the Decade to honour the best performers and performances in the previous 10 years.

ICC TV

ICC TV's vision is to create and provide credible, informative and engaging live and non-live content, that speaks to a global audience, attracts new fans and in the long term helps position Cricket as the "World's Favourite Sport"

ICC GLOBAL CRICKET ACADEMY

ICC Global Cricket Academy (GCA) is located at **Dubai Sports City** in the **United Arab Emirates**. The GCA's facilities include two ovals, each with 10 turf pitches, outdoor turf and synthetic practice facilities, indoor practice facilities including hawk eye technology and a cricket-specific gymnasium.

BCCI

The **Board of Control for Cricket in India** (**BCCI**) is the national governing body of Cricket in India. Its headquarters is situated at the Cricket centre in Churchgate, Mumbai. The BCCI is the wealthiest governing body of cricket in the world.

The BCCI was formed in December 1928 and is a consortium of state cricket associations that select their own representatives who elect the BCCI president.

As of February 2023, Roger Binny is the incumbent BCCI president and Jay Shah is the secretary.

The BCCI is an autonomous, private organisation that does not fall under the purview of the National Sports Federation of India and the Government of India has minimal regulation on it. It does not receive any grants or funds from the Ministry of Youth affairs and Sports.

The BCCI is influential in international cricket. The International Cricket Council shares the largest part of its revenue with the BCCI.

ICC Recognizes BCCI as Representative of India since 1928.

BCCI is a private body. As per ICC, all sports bodies must be independent and autonomous and must not be under the control of the government.

BCCI is registered as per the Tamil Nadu societies registration act in Chennai and is a registered society.

The officials and players are paid salary and playing fees respectively from the money BCCI earns.

BCCI also conducts Ranji Trophy, Deodhar Trophy, Vijay Hazare Trophy, Irani Trophy, Duleep Trophy and NKP Salve Challenger Trophy, Syed Mushtaq Ali Trophy, Vinoo Mankad Trophy, Nayudu Trophy, Cooch Behar Trophy, Women's Senior One Day Trophy, Senior Women's T20 Trophy.

BCCI nurtures cricket at all levels.

BCCI REVENUE

The BCCI is the richest cricket board in the world. This revenue comes from a variety of sources.

Media Rights

Official kit sponsorship rights.

Ticket price for all International and domestic matches.

Advertising related revenue.

Price money that Indian team obtains in tours and fixtures.

Title Sponsorship

Team Sponsorship

Revenue Earned via Bilateral Series

Revenues from the Indian Premier League

Franchisee consideration

ICC share distributions

Revenue from International Tours

Revenue from IPL

Champions league income

Interest from bank

BCCI PAY PACKAGE

BCCI is the richest cricket body in the world and it definitely looks after the players handsomely.

Indian cricketers are among the top paid players in world cricket.

An Indian player with a Grade A+ contract earns Rs 7 crores per year.
An Indian player with a Grade A contract earns Rs 5 crores per year.
An Indian player with a Grade B contract earns Rs 3 crores per year.
An Indian player with a Grade C contract earns Rs 1 crore per year.

This is a fixed amount and a player draws this money irrespective of the number of games he plays.

INDIAN PLAYERS = GRADE A+ = ROHIT SHARMA, VIRAT KOHLI, JASPRIT BUMRAH, RAVINDRA JADEJA.

INDIAN PLAYERS = GRADE A = HARDIK PANDYA, R ASHWIN, MD SHAMI, RISHABH PANT, AXAR PATEL.

INDIAN PLAYERS = GRADE B = CHATESHWAR PUJARA, KL RAHUL, SHREYAS IYER, MD SIRAJ, SURYAKUMAR YADAV, SHUBNAM GILL

INDIAN PLAYERS = GRADE C = UMESH YADAV, SHIKHAR DHAWAN, SHARDUL THAKUR, ISHAN KISHAN, DEEPAK HOODA, YUZVENDRA CHAHAL, KULDEEP YADAV, WASHINGTON SUNDAR, SANJU SAMSON, ARSHDEEP SINGH, KS BHARAT

For a TEST MATCH, Indian player earns Rs 15 lakhs or 7.5 lakhs if not included in playing XI

For an ODI, Indian player earns Rs 6 lakh or 3 lakhs if not included in playing XI

For an T20I, Indian player earns Rs 3 lakh or 1.5 lakhs if not included in playing XI.

There is also a 'bonus money' (this is over and above match fee) that an India cricketer draws as a reward for match winning performance.
Century = Rs 5 lakhs Bonus
Double Century = Rs 7 lakhs Bonus
5 Wickets = Rs 5 Lakhs Bonus

CRICKET GROUNDS REVENUE

Usually, Cricket grounds are owned by respective state or city associations recognised by BCCI.

Each State association has a set of office bearers, who run and manage the grounds.

There are certain grounds like Brabourne stadium in Mumbai, which is owned and managed by BCCI.

There are a few private stadiums that have come up like the D Y Patil Stadium in Mumbai, sometimes they are cheaper than association grounds.

Each state association can have one or more stadiums like the Karnataka State Cricket Association have their ground in Bangalore, Alur (outskirts of Bangalore), Mysore, Shivamogga, Hubbali and more.

For the matches conducted by BCCI, like the tests match, ODI and T20, other than IPL, the entire gate collection and In Stadia Advertisement money goes to the respective state association. Apart from this revenue, the organising state association gets organising fees from BCCI. The amount that the BCCI earns from selling TV rights, Sponsorships etc, is also shared with the respective state associations.

The test hosting centres like Mumbai, Chennai, Bangalore, Delhi, Kolkata etc get more share than the non-test hosing centres like say, Kerala, Goa, Bihar etc.

In case of IPL, where the teams are franchises, the cricket ground during the course of IPL "belongs to them". Franchises are in charge of the ground and they get the revenue generated through ticket sales, In-Stadia advertisements etc. The respective State association, where the IPL matches are held, get ground fees or rent from the Franchisee. BCCI also shares the IPL revenue generated through sponsorship and TV rights with these association.

The wicket and the outfield during IPL matches are managed by the respective state association.

Cricket grounds are also rented out for other sporting events or musical concerts or private functions like marriage.

Building and Maintaining a CRICKET GROUND is expensive and challenging.

ADVERTISERS LOVE CRICKET

The gap between every over makes a huge difference. No other SPORT can boast of this time gap. In each match 20 batsmen have to be given out or sent back to pavilion.

In a 50 overs per side game, 50 ads per team = 100 ads + 20 outs = maximum 120 advertisement slots are possible. It depends on the how the game is shaping up. The beauty is, no other game has this possibility, and that's the MAGIC OF CRICKET and THIS IS BIG MONEY maybe the BIGGEST ANY SPORT CAN DEMAND FOR.

Each game session is 3hrs30minutes=210 minutes= 50 advertisements per session = 210/50 = session time (**divide by**) no of overs = an advertisement opportunity every 4.2minutes = possibility of an advertisement every 252 seconds = **no other game can challenge this opportunity.**

2 SESSIONS PER MATCH

Bonus advertisements slots available when every batsman is out.

Cricket can become world's favourite sport, the adv opportunity is the magnet to attract every major company in the world to be part of global cricket.

ACKNOWLEDGEMENTS

All information in this eBook is extracted from

1) ICC world cup website
2) BCCI website
3) News Feed on internet
4) Wikipedia
5) Quora
6) If any Individual or group or any associations or any organisations or institutions feels that any content here belongs to them originally, do let me know and I will add your name details here in the acknowledgement section.

www.ingramcontent.com/pod-product-compliance
Lightning Source LLC
LaVergne TN
LVHW090132160826
845673LV00017B/2444
* 9 7 9 8 8 9 1 3 3 5 7 7 6 *